ELLIE
& JACK

Third Grade Ghost Hunters

Dedication Page

To my family, who had no idea I was writing this book. In fact, they probably thought I was just hanging out in my room downstairs to get some peace and quiet.

And now in the future, I can use the excuse that I am writing another book just to hang out in my room downstairs to get some peace and quiet.

It's a win-win for all of us.

Jack

My name's Jack. My sister's name is Ellie. We are twins and have been together, for better or worse, every day of our lives. Mom and Dad said they were only expecting one of us so we basically have to share everything.

That is why we have to share our bedroom and I have to put up
with Frozen posters on the wall.

We are both eight years old, but Ellie likes to act like the boss all the time. She thinks she is so much smarter than me just because she was born ten minutes earlier than I was. I was probably just being nice when we were being born and let her go first because that is what boys are supposed to do with girls.

We don't have any other brothers and sisters, so Mom says it is important that we always get along. We do have a couple of pets that are part of the family. Smoosh is our Shitsu dog that we have had for about five years. (Mom doesn't like it when we say the word Shitsu. My Dad usually laughs.) He got the name Smoosh because when we adopted him from the shelter, he would always smoosh his face into his food and water. We also have a cat Charlotte that Ellie named. All in all, our family is pretty great.

Ellie

Hi there! My name is Ellie and I understand that you have already heard from my brother Jack. We are twins, but I don't think we look anything alike. After all, I have blondish-brown hair and he has brownish-blonde hair. Plus, he probably won't admit this, but I am like an inch taller than he is. Did he tell you that we share a bedroom?

He probably complained about my Frozen posters, but he has wrestling posters on the wall. I don't mind John Cena and the Rock (who kind of looks like my Dad), however, do these posters have to be so close to my bed?

Jack thinks I'm bossy and says I think I am smarter than he is. I don't think I am smarter than he is.

I know I am smarter than he is. I get all A's in school and he usually gets B's or sometimes even C's. The truth is he could get all A's, too, but he doesn't always seem too interested in class.

Dad says we only have each other though, so we have to make the best of it. My Dad and Mom are my heroes. My Mom is so smart and not boring at all like many smart people are. Dad makes us laugh every single day and always has time for us. Besides Jack, Dad, and Mom, we have Smoosh and Charlotte in our family as well. Charlotte is our newest addition. She is a kitten and I got to name her Charlotte after my favorite book Charlotte's Web.

Jack

We live in a small town called Lake Thunderbird. Mom and Dad say it is one of the most peaceful places in the world. I don't know about that since I really haven't traveled more than an hour away from home, but it seems pretty nice. It's not too crowded and there are plenty of woods to explore.

Ellie

Dad grew up in Lake Thunderbird when he was a kid, so he wants us to experience the same thing he did. It really is a pretty cool place to live. In fact, there is nothing I don't like about Lake Thunderbird. Well...maybe just one thing.

Jack

Ellie is scared of the house next door to us. Dad said that no one has lived there in the last twenty years. It is kind of a big house, but now there are some windows broken and it definitely needs to be painted. At night, when we walk past it, Ellie always holds her breath and hurries. She doesn't think I notice, but I do.

Ellie

That house is spooky! I swear sometimes I have seen someone looking out from all of those broken windows. But Dad says no one has lived there forever, so it has to be a ghost. Mom tells me all the time there is no such thing as ghosts. Dad believes in ghosts though.

Jack

Mom doesn't believe in ghosts one bit. Dad does. When Mom says there is no such thing as ghosts, Dad waits until she leaves the room and tells us there are definitely ghosts in this world. I think he waits until Mom is out of the room because Mom gives him an angry look when we talk about ghosts. I'm not sure if Dad is scared of ghosts, but he seems to be awfully scared of Mom.

Ellie

If there is one thing Jack and I love to do it is to solve mysteries. Just last week we solved the mystery of why all of those cookies were disappearing from the cookie jar on the counter.

Jack

Mom and Dad said they both had no idea where all of those cookies were going. And we knew that Smoosh and Charlotte were not eating them. So we hid underneath the kitchen table for hours one night in the dark kitchen and we saw Mom getting cookies out of the jar three times. Each time she took two cookies.

Ellie

When we told Dad that Mom was the one taking the cookies every night, he smiled and asked how we figured it out. Jack and I told him and he laughed.

Jack

I didn't see anything funny about it! Mom was stealing six cookies a night. When we asked Dad how we should tell Mom that we knew it was her, he started shaking his head.

Ellie

Dad said that sometimes it is best to not say anything at all. We might make her embarrassed or hurt her feelings.

Jack

That's what Dad said, but I still wrote her a note and put it in the cookie jar. The note said that I knew it was her that was taking the cookies at night. I even signed my name. That night, Mom woke both Ellie and me up in the middle of the night smiling and gave us each a cookie for being such good detectives.

I know it was Mom who was taking cookies at night.

Jack.

Ellie
I've never had a better cookie in my life! Dad watched from the bedroom door and was smiling, too.

Jack
Now I am trying to convince Ellie that we should go ahead and try solving the mystery of the haunted house next door to us. I know she is scared of ghosts, but I want to find out what is really going on in there.

-X-

-CHAPTER 2-

Ghost Hunting Time

Jack
We have enough batteries for our flashlights now to last the rest of our lives.

Ellie
As I always tell Jack, you can never be too prepared. And I don't like the dark.

Jack
I had to convince Ellie not to tell Mom and Dad about our investigation. It wasn't easy. We are just going to be next door, so if anything goes wrong, we can run back to our house in seconds.

Ellie
Jack acts a lot braver than he actually is. If we see a ghost or something even a little scary, he won't wait around. He will run back home without me in a second. He'd probably even hide underneath his bed.

Jack
Ellie told you that I hide under my bed when I am scared? That's not true! Well... maybe it happened once. But it was a really bad thunderstorm with a lot of lightning.

Ellie
Seeing Smoosh and Jack cuddling under his bed during the storm was priceless.

Jack

It has been almost impossible to find the right moment to look around that house next door. We are in the middle of our summer vacation from school so you would think we would have time.

Ellie

Dad works from home some days and is out elsewhere on other days. He is a writer and keeps pretty busy, but he still always has time for us. Mom is actually a doctor and has her moments of being gone for lengthy periods of time. It comes with the job though.

Jack

Dad likes to call Mom our Sugar Momma because she makes more money than he does. Mom says it is not polite to talk about money. Anyway, they still treat us like babies sometimes. When they are both gone from the house, they usually ask our Grandma to watch us at our house. That's what happened today.

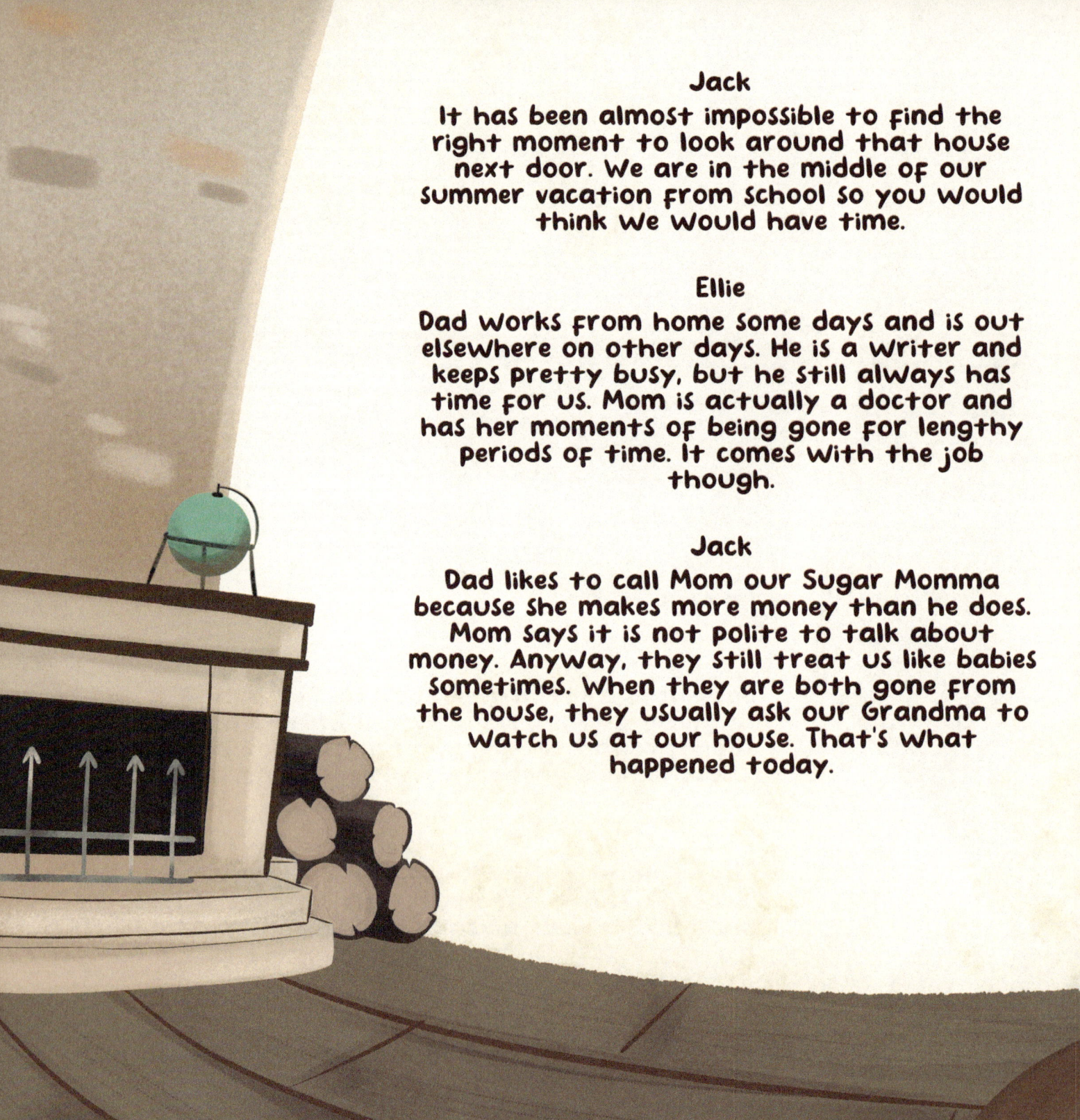

Ellie
Grandma has developed a habit of falling asleep not long after she sits down in our recliner in the living room. After some careful planning, we had grandma sitting down in that chair.

Jack

We asked her to help us with a puzzle that has like a thousand pieces. I hate puzzles, but Ellie is pretty good at them. Don't tell her I said that.

Ellie
Grandma fell asleep within ten minutes.

Jack
She snores louder than Dad. And it looks like her teeth are going to pop out of her mouth when she is sleeping. Dad told us those are called dentures. Fake teeth. Mom says it is not polite to talk about Grandma's fake teeth.

Ellie
At this point, we grabbed our supplies and headed outside.

Jack
We walked around that house with our flashlights and juice boxes for twenty minutes.

Ellie
I also had a notepad with us to take down any important notes. Dad taught us that is what reporters do.

Jack
The flashlights didn't really do us any good since it was about noon and the sun was shining down on top of us. I was sweating through my shirt.

Ellie
Jack sweats like an old man already. Mom says I can keep cool even in the desert.

Jack
We just walked around the house a few times looking closely at things.

Ellie
One time the mailman walked by on the sidewalk and we hid behind a bush.

Jack
Ellie almost freaked out. She thought he had seen us. She worries like that. What's the mailman going to do anyway? He is paid to deliver mail. Not yell at kids.

Ellie
Jack should worry more.

Jack

All we saw the entire time as we investigated the outside of the house was paint flaking off the siding. There were a few broken windows, but it was way too dark inside to see what was on the inside of the house.

Ellie

Other than the juice boxes tasting so good, it was kind of a waste of time. Jack drank five of them and went to the bathroom on a tree in the backyard. Boys!

Jack

If you are going to be a successful ghost hunter, you really should look inside the house.

Ellie
Jack kept on saying he wanted us to climb in through one of those broken windows, but Grandma could have woken up at any time.

-X-

-CHAPTER 3-

Operation: Night Time Ghost Hunting

Jack

So we had an idea. Once Mom and Dad tucked us in for the night, we were going to come back to the house and actually go inside. We would put those flashlights to work!

Ellie

Jack came up with the idea of going into the house after dark. Our bedtime is nine at night. He wants us to climb out of our bedroom window and go sneak around in the dark.

Jack

We're on the first floor so it's not like we are high up.

Ellie

Jack always has really bad ideas. (He once tried to make dinner as a surprise for our parents and those Pop-Tarts almost burned down the house.) I only agreed with it because I knew he would do it with or without me. I'm his older sister. I need to take care of him.

Jack

We both went to bed that night in our gray sweatpants and dark shirts. We would blend in with the dark so people (and maybe ghosts) wouldn't be able to see us.

Ellie

I wanted to wear something bright yellow with reflectors attached to it, but Jack said we could get busted if people saw us and get in big trouble. I'm more worried about ghosts than prison time.

Jack

Mom and Dad didn't suspect a thing. We acted like we were sleepy, yawned a few times, and then after they tucked us in and did the whole "We love you" bit, we asked for them to close our bedroom door.

Ellie

I love that they tuck us in every night. If we ask really nicely, they tell us a story lots of times. Tonight I caught myself and stopped from asking them otherwise we probably would have fallen asleep and missed our investigation.

Ellie

The first part of the plan went well. It even sounded like Mom and Dad went to bed not more than ten minutes after us. This is when we went to the window and tried to climb out.

Jack

I had removed the screen earlier in the day so it would be out of the way.

Ellie

Jack is pretty handy with his hands. He may not be as good as me at school, but he can build things out of nothing. It took him no time at all to remove that screen.

Jack

The jump down from our window was only a few feet.

Ellie

But a few feet in the dark might as well be thirty feet. You can't see well enough to know when your feet are going to hit the ground.

Jack

Is Ellie making excuses? Yep. She fell when she jumped down from our window. Totally bit it. She even made a little bit of a yell. I thought for sure we would see Mom and Dad's bedroom light fly on.

Ellie

I muffled my cry as best as I could... even though I thought I broke my ankle.

Jack

Ellie said she broke her ankle and then limped for about ten seconds. Ellie didn't even sprain her ankle, let alone break it.

Ellie

Anyway, we were over to the house next door in seconds. It is strange how your neighborhood can look so friendly during the day and so scary at night. If Jack wasn't with me, I probably would have turned around and climbed right back into our bedroom window.

Jack

Don't tell Ellie this, but our neighborhood is spooky at night! Sometimes Dad will ask me to walk Smoosh in our backyard at night so he can go to the bathroom before going to sleep. I hold my breath the entire time and listen to many of the weird sounds going on close by. Sometimes I think aliens or werewolves will come out from behind the trees and take us.

Ellie

I'm not sure you have ever had someone try pushing you through a broken window, but it didn't go smoothly. Jack tried helping me into the house next door but I think I am stronger than he is. I finally just pulled myself up.

Jack
I give Ellie credit. She went into the dark house first.

Ellie
I probably went through a hundred spider webs once I went through that broken window. I was not happy. But I was too scared to complain.

Jack
Once I pulled myself inside, we turned on our flashlights. You would not believe what we saw in there!

Ellie
Whoever lived there last must have left all of their things. The house had furniture and everything. It was just covered with dust, dirt, and cobwebs.

Jack

Do you know why all of their things were left behind? Probably because somebody died there. You can't take your things with you on that trip! I don't think Ellie figured these things out.

Ellie

I didn't want to tell Jack that the reason all the furniture and everything was still there was because someone almost certainly passed away there. I could tell he was already scared and I didn't want to make things worse.

Jack

The room that we climbed into was the living room. There were still pictures on the wall. When we shined our flashlights at them, most of them were pictures of old people.

VII-XI
MCMXXIV

Ellie
Being in the dark was a bit frightening, but nothing was jumping out at us so we decided to go to the next room. It was the kitchen. Jack decided that we should sit down at the kitchen table and listen quietly.

Jack

I wanted to see if we could hear any strange noises coming from anywhere inside the house. If there was a ghost, shouldn't we hear something? I thought it was a great idea... until we heard a sound coming from the upstairs.

Ellie

I think my heart stopped for a full minute.

Jack

I almost went to the bathroom in my sweatpants.

Ellie

I think Jack almost pooped his pants.

Jack

I guess Ellie should have brought an air freshener in her supplies.

Ellie
It sounded like someone or something was moving around upstairs. I wanted to run back home as quickly as possible.

Jack
Did I mention I almost pooped my pants?

Ellie
But then I remembered. We were doing this ghost hunting investigation because of me! Jack was here trying to help me figure out what I had seen in the windows those few times in the past. I felt like I owed it to him to be brave.

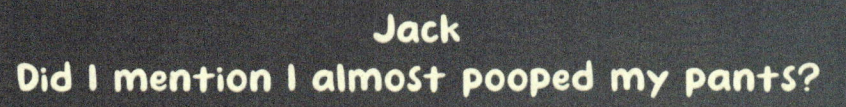

Jack
We slowly climbed up the stairs. It seemed like it took forever.

Ellie
It took forever climbing up those stairs because I had to almost drag Jack up every step. He wasn't in a hurry to find out what was making those noises.

Jack

Did Ellie tell you she was pulling me up the stairs? That's not true! I was just trying to plan an exit strategy. If we found something upstairs that was truly terrifying, I wanted to be able to run out of there in the dark as quickly as possible.

-CHAPTER 4-

The Dark Hallway

Ellie

We chose to investigate the bedrooms only and not the bathroom.

Jack

The last thing I wanted to do was check out a stinky, old bathroom. We kept that door closed. How many ghosts do you know that use the bathroom anyway?

Ellie

The first bedroom was so dark even with our flashlights it took several moments for our eyes to adjust. It was just an old bed with a dresser.

Jack

There was a closet in the room as well. I held my breath as I opened it.

Ellie

I thought Jack was going to faint. I didn't hear him breathing at all.

Jack

In that closet, all I saw were old dresses that were really out of style. I even moved some of the dresses off to the side to see if anything was behind them, but there was nothing.

Jack
We both shone our flashlights as we made our way to the other bedroom upstairs. The door creaked open as we gently pushed on it.

Ellie
The door gave this loud and long "Crrrrreeeaaaakkk!" as we opened it. My heart stopped. I figured everything in the house and everyone in the neighborhood probably heard it.

Jack
In this bedroom was a really large bed and a couple of dressers.

Ellie

The bed was big like the one in Mom and Dad's bedroom at home. Jack said a married couple must have lived there. Or someone really fat that needed an extra-large bed. Now that I think back, that joke was pretty funny.

Jack

I like trying to make my sister laugh. It makes me feel good. Don't tell her I said that though.

Ellie

Jack is the funniest kid in class. He's never boring. That is for sure!

Jack

When it came time to open up the closet in this bedroom, I let Ellie take the lead.

Ellie

I figured since Jack opened the last closet, I might as well open this one.

Jack

I was hoping there would be a dancing skeleton in the closet when Ellie opened it up, but instead there were just some clothes and boxes. It would have been pretty sweet to see Ellie's eyes pop out of her head if there was a dancing skeleton.

Ellie

So far, our night time ghost hunting investigation had turned up nothing.

-X-

-CHAPTER 5-

Mysterious Guests

Ellie
Right as I was telling Jack that our investigation was a failure, we heard it.

Jack
There was a sound that came from close by. It sounded like a thud.

Ellie
Like a book or something dropped to the floor. We stood there silently with our flashlights shining as we waited for another sound.

Jack

All I could hear were Ellie's teeth chattering away. She was scared! I almost felt bad for her.

Ellie

Jack may tell you that my teeth were chattering because I was scared. Well... it was a bit chilly in the house as well!

Jack

That is when we heard it.

Ellie

Something was softly creeping towards us in the dark. It was coming straight down the hall and towards the bedroom we were in.

Jack

Don't tell Ellie this, but I thought about running out of their screaming. But I knew she would make fun of me the rest of our lives if I did.

Ellie

If I wasn't Jack's big sister, I probably would have left him there and jumped out the window on the second floor. I had never been so scared.

Jack

We had our flashlights pointed at the open bedroom door and that is when we saw it...

Ellie

Two glaring eyes were peering in at us. They glowed in the dark!

Jack
We both gasped for a second. But then I noticed the eyes were pretty low to the floor. Like a short baby.

Ellie
Jack whispered to me that it was a short baby that was glaring in at us with glowing eyes. I immediately filed that away in my brain of comments to ignore.

Jack
As our eyes adjusted a bit better, we saw what it was. Or more like who it was!

Ellie
Charlotte nearly gave us a heart attack!

Jack

Our cat Charlotte must have been treating this house like her own personal playground.

Ellie

It made perfect sense! Charlotte probably catches a ton of mice in here. All of those times when I thought the eyes of a ghost were looking out at me, it was just Charlotte watching me walk by the house.

Jack

Cats are sometimes weird like that. If Smoosh would see us, he would come running and lick our faces. Cats seem like they ignore us half the time. Dad likes to say cats are more independent.

Ellie

Mom has always said that Charlotte probably has a whole other life that we don't know about. Charlotte always disappears outside a few hours a day and most of the night. Now we know where she has been going.

Jack
I patted Charlotte on her head as she purred and told her we won't tell on her if she doesn't tell on us.

Ellie
I'm not sure if Charlotte understood our agreement, but she acted like she did. I decided to scoop her up and bring her back home with us.

-X-

-CHAPTER 6-

The Most Scared
I Have Ever Been in My Life

Jack
We were just getting down to the end of the dark staircase when we heard footsteps.

Ellie
These weren't soft cat footsteps either. These were loud, ghost-like footsteps.

Jack
As we stood there in the dark holding our breath and clutching Charlotte like she was going to protect us, the footsteps got closer.

Ellie
It was right at this moment that both of our flashlights started to fade.

Jack
I guess Ellie had bought old "new" batteries. They must have been sitting on the shelf in the store for years because these batteries were dead. I was just hoping we wouldn't be following them into the afterlife quite yet!

Ellie
I am going to return those batteries to the store! I saved the receipt.

Jack
The heavy footsteps were just about on top of us. Whatever it was... it was very close! And now that it was completely dark, we couldn't see a thing.

Ellie
Don't say anything to Jack because I know he will get embarrassed. But he actually took a step and stood in front of me as the "thing in the dark" was coming our way. He was trying to protect me. I'll always love him for that. But again, if you say anything to him about this, I will deny it.

Jack
And then we heard the "thing in the dark" call out to us. It said "Jack and Ellie" in a sort of quiet and deep way!

Ellie
It took me a moment to recognize the voice, but once I did, I realized quickly that I probably would have wanted it to be a ghost instead.

Jack
A blinding light hit us. As our eyes adjusted, we saw that it was Dad shining his flashlight at us.

Ellie
He was not happy.

Jack
He asked what we were doing in the abandoned house next door at 11 at night. He was M-A-D. Dad said if we thought he was angry, just wait until Mom hears about this.

Ellie
Once I blurted out in one breath that we were investigating the house for ghosts, he got a worried look on his face.

Jack
I may not be "book" smart, but I am "people" smart. I can tell what people are thinking by the looks on their faces.

Ellie
Jack explained to me later that Dad would also be in trouble with Mom because he has always told us ghosts are real. If Mom heard about us being over there in the middle of the night, all three of us would be grounded! Actually, all four of us. Charlotte would never be let outside again.

Jack
We ended up making the same deal with Dad as we made with Charlotte. If he didn't tell Mom, then we wouldn't tell Mom either.

Ellie
Sneaking back outside and having to go through that broken window was quite an adventure with Dad. We actually all started giggling as Dad briefly became stuck in the window.

Jack
I think Dad was just joking around that he was stuck in the window. He told us that next time we were going to have to put a coat of butter on him so he could slide through the window easier.

Ellie

That's when I knew this was going to be one of those stories we would tell the rest of our lives when Mom left the room. Or at least until Jack and I are adults. She can't ground us when we have our own families.

Jack

Dad helped us back in our bedroom window and even tossed Charlotte inside the window as well. He said he had to finish his walk with Smoosh really quick and we had better be asleep by the time he checked on us.

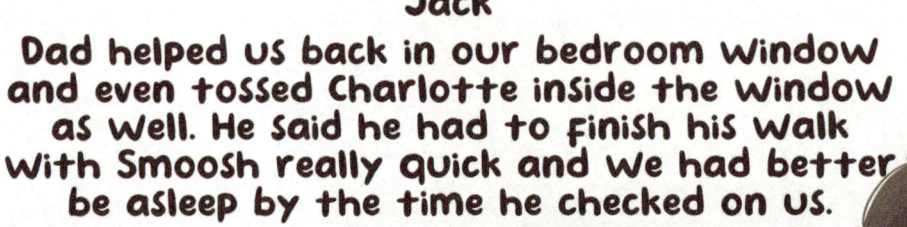

Ellie

Of course, we were way too excited to fall right asleep, so when Dad checked on us in a few minutes, we pretended we were sleeping.

Jack

I think Dad knew we were faking it.

Ellie
Of course Dad knew we were pretending to sleep because Jack does some really loud fake snoring when he is trying to act like he is catching some z's.

Jack
As Dad made sure our bedroom window was locked and closed our bedroom door, I heard him give a soft chuckle.

Ellie
Dad quietly closed our bedroom door and said, "Good night, my ghost hunters. You two (three counting Charlotte) are very brave. But let's not go into that scary abandoned house again please."

Jack
While we may not go back in that house to look for ghosts, I do have some other mysteries I'd like to solve.

Ellie
I think Jack and I are going to be having adventures together for the rest of our lives!

THE END

Printed in Great Britain
by Amazon